bat at yarn.

Kittens love…
to sit on the windowsill
for hours and hours
and watch birds.

Kittens love...
to roll in catnip,
walk on fences,
scramble up trees.

Kittens love to lie in a
heap and squirm and wrestle.

Kittens love to nap...
in a patch of sunlight,

on the Sunday paper,

in a basket of fresh laundry.

Kittens love to hunt...
for mice,
and bugs,
and butterflies.

And when everyone else is
fast asleep…
kittens love
to explore the dark.

Kittens love to sharpen their claws...
on the bark of trees,

on the nap of carpets,

on the brand-new drapes. No, no, kitty!

Kittens love to lap their milk
and keep their fur shiny clean.

Kittens love to hide in
paper bags. Boo!